Only Once Again
Short Stories

Renuka.K.P.

Ukiyoto Publishing

All global publishing rights are held by

Ukiyoto Publishing

Published in 2023

Content Copyright © Renuka.K.P.

ISBN 9789359207940

All rights reserved.

No part of this publication may be reproduced, transmitted, or stored in a retrieval system, in any form by any means, electronic, mechanical, photocopying, recording or otherwise, without the prior permission of the publisher.

The moral rights of the author have been asserted.

This is a work of fiction. Names, characters, businesses, places, events, locales, and incidents are either the products of the author's imagination or used in a fictitious manner. Any resemblance to actual persons, living or dead, or actual events is purely coincidental.

This book is sold subject to the condition that it shall not by way of trade or otherwise, be lent, resold, hired out or otherwise circulated, without the publisher's prior consent, in any form of binding or cover other than that in which it is published.

www.ukiyoto.com

In loving memories of my demised siblings

Contents

An Onam Celebration.	1
Kalariyakshi – A Fairy Tale.	7
Delusion.	12
A year-end Exam.	18
A Bangalore Trip.	23
A Chit Chat.	27
A Different Complacency.	32
Intercity.	37
Heaven and Hell.	44
About the Author	*47*

An Onam Celebration.

Today is Thiruvonam. The golden celebration in the golden Leo month! Uproars of celebrations are heard from all the sides around. Listening to all this Sudha was lying on the bed. After a deep breath, she got up slowly from there. Then came to the veranda and sat on the blue plastic chair in front of her small house. The chair where her mother had always used to sit. Sudha felt an indescribable relief when she sat on it.

By sitting there, the house of her elder brother who lives nearby to her home can be seen. She calls him Chetan. Chetan's wife Geetha's family had already come there the previous night itself to celebrate Onam with them.

After a while, Geetha's mother came down to the courtyard. Although Geetha is older than her by position, Sudha is calling her by name because they are of the same age. Geetha also prefers this as she wants to be younger always like most of the ladies here. When she saw her, Geetha's mother called out from there and asked.

"Why are you sitting idle there, come here instead of being there alone."

"Yes, Aunty, I am sitting idle here. When did Aunty come?" Sudha asked though she had known their arrival, just to ask something at that time.

"Your brother has invited us to celebrate onam here saying that to meet all. Don't be alone there, come here."

"Yes, I am coming."

After saying that, she went inside. What fate is she? She is invited by their guest to her own brother's house where she has the right to live with all her freedom, especially as she is unmarried and has no her own family. When Sudha remembered about it, she felt sad and disappointed inside. At that time there was a lizard making sound on the window pane telling what her thinking was correct.

If my mother was there! How well we could have celebrated Onam. Even after we both are alone, we prepared all the dishes for Onam and Vishu and enjoyed each festival. Usually, any of the elders would also give an Onakodi (a new dress for Onam) to both of us. Why did God call my mother so quickly by leaving me alone? How could she leave this earth peacefully by thinking about me? The reins of her thoughts slowly started to loosen and at last, it reached her mother.

I had no one to comfort me except my mother when I was deeply wounded in heart or depressed in agony.' She thought. ' When my mother left, how pathetic my life became in this house.' The memory of her beloved mother, who was her only support, began to make her emotional. That made her thoughts drift back to her childhood days.

After leaving school during the time of Onam, the first thing we did was to run to pick flowers with my younger sister and friends. The southern side of our ground was full of different colored flowers. We have to pick all these flowers up before Indu and Suma come from the next house. If we are seen in the ground picking flowers, Alice from the next house will also run to join us. Even though she doesn't make pookkalam (flower bed), she likes to enjoy picking flowers with us. There are full of kakkapoove (a small flower in the ground) everywhere... After picking kakkapoove and thumbapoove (a small white flower special to onam) in an okra leaf we will go home. it is enough to pick all the other flowers in the morning. The next morning, our pookkalam will be the best in that area. Remembering all these she sighed again.

One day they were picking kakkapoove from their neighbour Pillai's deserted ground. There was a pond in that deserted area. There are full of kakkappove all around it. Then there was a sound of 'boom' while they were picking flowers sitting there. Alice and her sister got frightened when they heard the sound.

"That's enough, let's go home," said the sister in a low voice. They said they saw a woman in the pond come up from the water.

She also heard the sound but when she looked, there was no one there. She thought that it must have been some illusion or something like that. But she could not believe that her sister and Alice said that they saw a female form rising from the water. Anyway, they returned home immediately and told the matter to her mom.

"Who told you to go near that pond? There is a ghost of a lady who died by drowning in that pond in the past."

"And the ghost, don't you just say it, Mother."She said.

"Savitri the neighbour in the east went to bathe in that pond immediately after she had come here after her wedding with Sundaran in that house. Later, do you want to hear what happened? Savitri was haunted by the ghost of that lady. Savitri began to talk just like that lady with whom she had no experience until then. It was Savitri's mother-in-law who realized that lady to whom she was familiar early. It should have seen Savitri's look at that time! Her voice and gestures were just like that lady according to her mother-in-law. Her eyes were shown with fear as red and changed. Seeing her everyone frightened." Her mother continued.

After hearing so much about it, they started shaking with fear. Her sister stood close to her mother with fear. Mother again said that the lady had been cheated by a Kumaran, and she had been conceived by him. So, she left this world by drowning in the pond and the two souls who had drowned were wandering there without getting a rebirth.

"That ghost is still there. Don't go there." Mother warned again.

Finally, at dusk, my mother took some salt and pepper in her hand and rounded over our heads. Then she put it in a fire and burned it to remove any negative vibration caught in us. My father made fun of Mother when he saw all this.

"What are you crazy about, any coconut must have fallen in that pond." Mother did not say much after that. Sudha is still remembering all these clearly.

Oh! How caring was my mother? If she were here today! Now I am alone in this house on this special Thiruvonnam day. Tears started flowing from her eyes without breaking as she remembered. Wherever my mother's soul is, she might be shedding tears remembering me'. Sudha heaved a sigh, thinking like this. At that time her brother came to her.

"What are you worried about? Why all these tears on your face?" He asked.

"Nothing, I suddenly remembered our mother."

"What's the matter in saying that now, she left?." His face also withered a little. Then he regained his balance of mind and said,

"Sudha, come over there, we can have food from there." She shook her head.

In Chetan's house, it is heard that Geetha and their guests are talking loudly and laughing by making somewhat jokes, etc. They are enjoying happily all together. Chetan wants me to join their group. But Geetha? She is saying that I am not mentally well. Then how can she allow me to join with them? She sighed again.

What happened to her life? The death of her father and the following insecurity at home, all these things had made some changes in her. Her mental state changed. She could not pass her exams. Some illusions, sometimes in the same posture for long periods without a word. If someone questions her, she will explode. Finally, a life addicted to pills.

The loneliness made her thoughtful and sad on this special occasion today. She thought. 'Although there is nothing wrong with me now, Geetha thinks that I am just crazy. How can they add me to them? If it were her sister in my place her attitude might be entirely different!'

As we know a person who has recovered from any mental disorder in his lifetime, will not be accepted by anyone as before even if how much they is innocent, except his family.

Sudha is afraid of Geetha. Her brother also fears her nature. If there is any dispute between them, by blackmailing or threatening him, she will put everything under her control. If it is not worked out, she will make the scene worse. Anyway, she is lucky as her husband is proud and self-respecting and he will hide everything without knowing others. The fact is that Sudha has medicine for her illness if any. But what about Geetha? No one knows about her behavioral disorder and how dangerous she is to his family.

"Sudha come and let's drink tea." Geetha's mother called again generously.

Sudha went inside without hearing it. She lay down lazily on the bed for a while. She fell asleep thinking about how she was being punished by God for which crime she had committed. When she gets up, it can be heard the noise of talking loudly from the north side of her home. Ammalu Amma, her children, and grandchildren are gathered on the veranda of her house there. One of her daughters lives with her. Another son is also living near it in another house. If there is any celebration or anything like that, they all gather together with her there. Then there will be like throwing a stone in the crow's nest. Sudha got up and opened the window on the north side and stood looking there for a while.

'If my marriage had taken place at the proper age, children like those would have been here as well. What can I say other than my destiny?' She felt sad again thinking like this. While looking out like that, her brother came there again.

"Sudha, haven't you taken a bath? Immediately have a bath and come home and have your tea there."

Poor man, he has come back restless after thinking about her. She then did some household duties like cleaning, and bathing, and went to Chetan's house.

"This onamkodi is for you." Geetha took a new dress and gave Sudha. She received it, thinking that whatever maybe it was enough for me.

Geetha will get a bonus and advance from the government. When she went there, they were discussing onam shopping. She did not want to hear about it. What is the matter to a cat at a place where the gold is kept? Onam is for people who have relatives and money. For people like her, it's like saying,' even if there is an onam or birthday come, the porridge for Koran will be always in a clay pot itself'. Aren't they marginalizing her? She had studied well in every class and might have reached high if she had not been ill. If anyone talks like this about her, Geetha will humiliate her saying she would have been a collector here.

Sudha sat on a chair in the dining room. Geetha's parents and brothers with their family are there. They are running here and there to make a feast etc. Sudha sat silently on one side of the table and had her breakfast alone. Then her brother came and sat near to her to give her company and began to talk something.

Sudha peeked into the kitchen. The cooking is going on well there. Some tasty smell is coming out. As she is not allowed in the kitchen by Geetha she didn't get in. Some of the guests asked her about something. Sudha replied to them and went home again.

Sudha knows very well that Geetha's non-cooperation makes her brother helpless. So, she often tries to keep away from them to save her brother from this helplessness. She prepares food for her alone. Only today she received a special invitation for Onam from Geetha. As her mind is not well, no one except her own family will accept her. She knew it well and calmed herself. After some time, she saw Chetan cutting the banana leaf from the backyard for a serving feast and taking it inside. Sudha went there again to have an Onam feast for which she had been invited by his brother earlier.

Though she has been prevented from putting pookkalam in these ten days Geetha showed some generosity by allowing her to join with them for the feast on this thiruvonam day. Sudha considers this itself as her good luck.

....

Kalariyakshi – A Fairy Tale.

"Walk fast without saying a word, don't look back." Kutettan told us in a low voice. We were going to Mattappadam (a place for exchanging goods with one another) holding his hand. My uncle has entrusted some money to him to spend for us. We are very happy and are excited about that.

When I asked 'What happened?', he told us not to speak by gesture showing his mouth covered with his hand and quickly put his feet forward and started walking with fear. After some time when they reached a certain place, Kuttettan(a brother from a nearby home) explained to us what had happened.

"Isn't that the way we just walked now? There is a Kalari inside the fence on the north side of that way. It is said that there is a fairy in that Kalari. A female figure with all her hair loose and wearing a white sari. At noon, she will come behind the passers-by and will ask for a little lime. When we turn around, we will see a Yakshi with long teeth, etc. as if waiting to drink our blood. Many people say that they have seen it."

When Kuttettan said this, there was fear in those eyes. Hearing the stories that many people were shocked to see the fairy, we reached Mattappadam.

In the past, before the invention of coins, there was a system of exchange of products. Instead of money, goods were used to exchange with each other for their transactions in those days. As a remnant of that, even today, every year in Chendamangalam, a place in Ernakulam district a trade fair is held on the day before the festival 'Vishu'. Kuttettan took us all over there and showed us everything. There are all kinds of ancient things like baskets, pots, mats, earthenware pots, and all such things. Kuttettan bought me a toy boat that runs on the water. My younger brother who is with us got a toy car and a flute. After wandering here and there, we returned with a lot of toys, watermelons, sweets, etc. On the way, we asked Kuttettan to return in another way.

"Kuttetta, we can return in another way. We are afraid of that fairy on the way." No one hid the fear.

'There is no other way. We need to fear only when we go alone at noon. Don't be afraid now." Kuttettan calmed us down. So we reached home.

Immediately after closing school in mid-summer, we were usually sent away from our home in the next town to celebrate the holidays at our mother's ancestral house in Chendamangalam every year. This time we came here from our home on foot two days before. We have to cross two rivers in ferry boats to reach here. We will walk frightened until we cross the ferry. After crossing the river, we will become excited and happy to reach the mother's home.

Our Grandmother passed away some years before and then one of our cousins was decided by her family to reside there to look after that house and the two uncles who were then bachelors there.. The uncles were very strict there. All the nephews had been very much feared and respected them. That's why there was very discipline in that house especially when they are in. Whenever we were there, we were used to talking to each other in a very low voice without making any kind of sound. Our veneration towards them was like that we even feared to ask anything repeatedly if we could not understand what they told us. Children from the neighbouring house in the north also come to stay with the cousin sister until both of them reach home in the evening in all days.

Kuttetten went to his home after dropping us here and the next day in the morning itself he reached again. The uncle had entrusted him earlier to go shopping as and when necessary. One day when he went to the ration shop, he took me with him. The way was through the front of an old Christian house called Anelil. I had gone earlier there to collect anchovy seeds with a friend from the neighbouring house in the east. When we reached near to that house, Kutettan, showed an old lady in that bungalow in the middle of that big ground.

"That grandmother did not die even after the priest came and gave her the last kudasa."

"Is that grandmother a ghost?" My doubt was misunderstood by him. Kuttettan did not like that question.

"Ah, I don't know about that," he said resentfully.

We walked telling the stories of how that grandma came back to life even after she was given the last rites.

There was a singer of the church who lived in the house on the south side next. His daughter Gressy was of my age but she would not talk to me. She may have an ego as she is the younger daughter of that ancient Christian house with essential property. The women of that house were seldom seen outside. If we look from the road, we can see only the curtain plant hanging. An orthodox family. When I see her, I remember that rich girl Gressy who hesitated to share her umbrella with Lilly who went to school in the rain without an umbrella in the famous story of Muttathu Varki's 'Orukudayum Kunjupengalumm.'

After the demise of the grandmother, the elder uncle was mostly in prayer. The uncle who believed that his mother died due to someone's witchcraft has resorted to bhakti to get rid of its bad effects hereafter. He will wake up at four o'clock in the morning and perform baths and rituals every day. We usually wake up in the morning hearing the chanting of Naamajapam and smelling the fragrance of sandalwood.

Staying there, one day a woman came there seeking help to write a petition. The younger uncle who is a school teacher took paper and pen and told me to write. I was in fifth grade and wrote what my uncle told me in good handwriting. It was a petition for her daughter to get a transfer certificate to change the school. When they were asking, 'Isn't this sir's sister's child?' my pride rose to the sky.

An LP school teacher who teaches children to write the first letters of language had been very much respected by the common people in the society at that time. I have heard that a college lecturer who was teaching political science in a college had thought about his LP school teacher as 'the greatest man' in his childhood. Those who teach the initial letters will always be remembered.

Kutettan always comes in the evening. Then in the room next to the kitchen, we all get together and talk about many things. One day during our talk, when he described how the end of the world would happen by showering fire, we all began to shiver with fear.

School is about to open. We have to go back home. Uncle gave us money for the bus fare. So we became happy and peaceful. There is no need to be afraid to get on the ferry. After taking a bath and having porridge we get ready to go home. Now, it is 11:30 am. We left home after saying farewell to our cousin sister and uncle. Oh my god, this way is the same as to Mattappadam. It was only then we reached there it was came to understand. The same way along the side of Kalary through which we went to Mattapadam. After the canal bridge, we reached the pathway. When we reached near Kalari we looked inside the fence on the north side fetching head with fear. It is noon? An old, dilapidated building resembling a small temple seen locked. Could this be the Kalari that Kutettan said? We got frightened. 'Let's go quickly.' After telling this secretly, we started walking quickly. Then a call was heard from behind. A woman's voice.

" Stay there."

We didn't see anyone for so long. How suddenly did she come? I slowly looked behind with half-closed eyes. Yes, it is a woman.

"Run...I also saw a figure with a white saree with spread hair". Then both of us ran without looking back till we got on the cement bench in the waiting shed of the bus stand. We were afraid even to speak to each other. At that time a sister came into the shed.

"Why did you run away when I called you? Are not sister Bhavani's children?"

"'Yes, we ran thinking it was time for the bus," I replied.

That sister belongs to our mother's family and knew all of us. Later when we reached home, we all laughed talking about this stupidness. Moreover, it came to know that she is unmarried and leading a life as a nun wearing white clothes and spreading hair with thulasikathir on her head. She is always in bhakti.

'I have been hearing that there is a fairy in that area for a long time, so it is better not to go that way at noon'. Mother's advice.

No matter how much we thought about why the Yakshi was living in Kalari, we did not get a clue.

....

Delusion.

It is a quarter past nine. The bus will arrive shortly. Jodsna hung her bag, locked the gate, and got out. Pulling the shawl straight on the shoulder she started running to the bus stop. If she gets this bus, she can reach the office on time. If you are late for a minute, then there is no chance of getting that bus. The superintendent in the office is waiting to reach 10 o'clock to mark late in the attendance book. She walked briskly. While walking she was trying to remember all the things to be done in the office. The audit was about to start. All the records have to be corrected. In the meantime, many people will come up with many demands. They should be answered.

"Why is Jodsna running even though it's Monday?"

She looked back with a smile. It is Basheerika from the next house. 'Why should he be worried whether I ran or walked', she thought in her mind. But she did not tell it to him and passed just a slight smile as an answer. So, she walked and reached the bus stop. Immediately when the bus arrived, she grabbed hold of it and got on it. There is no place to step on the bus.

'Kerioru kerioru keriniku'. ('All those who are stepped inside should move to the front) The cleaner of the bus is making noise by knocking on the side of the bus.

A 'Kili'(nickname of bus cleaner) that has no time to get the people in.

"Why do you try to break the bus?" Someone got angry with him.

He will ring the bell to start the bus before people get on board. If it is seen his noise and behavior, one may think that he is going to buy an emergency pill. It often seems that the government should give forcefully one more training to get self-control before giving licenses to drivers. Nowadays wherever we look in our country, a lot of awareness workers are seen.

When she comes back home from office work, it will be around 6 o'clock. Once she gets to rest for a while, she restarts her 'journey' to her household matters again. Then she stays doing all the work at home until she sleeps. As soon as the alarm goes off at dawn, Jodsna jumps up and spends two hours in the kitchen usually. Both her children are studying in an English medium school. Their school bus comes by 7:30 a.m. For her husband, he has to leave at 8 a.m. After preparing food for them and leaving them on time, she can sit quietly in her world alone for a while. Wow! It has been fifteen years since this journey began.

Jodsna's children study in the most famous school in the country. Her children were admitted to that school in LKG on the high recommendation of a senior official in her department. Jodsna and her husband had been initially denied admission because they could not speak English fluently. That's why Jodsna tried for the recommendation. How difficult it was for her! How much she tried for it!Shiva Shiva! The aim behind all this was an admission to entrance coaching class and thereby a professional course for their children in the future. Now we can get admission even in the coaching class if the students have high marks only! Jodsna has seen many people who work with her struggling for it. That's why she is taking precautions right now. She was surprised to see her friend bring her children to a small class of a school under a famous coaching institution to ensure admission there in the future. But Jodsna is now on the same path.

At that time, another Onam season came. As children have to go to school early in the morning, pookkalam is not made here. School time is not suitable for it and all are busy at that time. In any case, this year Jodsna decided to make pookkalam with available flowers there.

"Children, we should make Pookkalam this year, it's been a while since we made it in our yard on Onam."

"Oh, Mom should leave us alone. We have other works."Saying this they turned on the TV and began to watch cartoon serials.

'Atham' day (the first day of the celebration) arrived after some days. Jodsna didn't say anything to her children because she knew there was no time for them in the morning. The school bus would arrive at 7 o'clock itself.

When Onam season came in her childhood, she would go and pick flowers along with her friends from neighbouring homes. The yard would be cleaned using cow dung. An Aunt in the neighbouring home used to make flower bags out of palm leaves for everyone. At that time, it was enough to go to school at 10 o'clock and come back at 4 p.m. What a competition was there between friends to make the best pookkalam!

All kinds of flowers had been blooming on the fences of all the houses. At that time holidays were the happiest days. The boys from nearby homes with a stick in their hands would go on the road in groups to pick flowers from the houses on both sides of the road. It was especially happy and exciting to pick flowers from the top of the walls of some houses without knowing them as an adventure. There would be full of pea flowers in the nearby Sreemoolam club. The onam season was the days full of happiness and excitement in her childhood. But for her children.? It can be said that they see this pookkalam (flower beds) in the school only.

Jodsna is now going to work after picking some flowers from the yard and putting a pookkalam(flower bed) on the car porch as she had no dung to clean the yard. When she comes in the evening, Joyce will ask her children for their opinion about the flower bed.

'How was the flower bed, children?'

The children look like they have seen something stupid. They have never experienced the beauty of Onam in its real sense.

Immersed in the magical world created by the education vendors, she and her husband endured everything and are paying all the money they earned as fees to teach their children in English medium school. But now the disdain, the children are showing toward their unique culture is making her a little disappointed. Although there are not many facilities, she felt that government schools are much better for the internal growth and cultural upliftment of the children. She has seen the love and care of the nearby children shown each other on their way to govt. school. Many of those who have studied here have reached the highest levels of society. When her husband came in the evening, she talked about her disappointment.

"Don't you do all these seeing your friends? you must suffer it all alone. On the one side losing our money and on the other side changing their culture. Aren't all these things done by you only, the n why this tear?'. He became furious.

". Let me say one more thing. If this goes like this, after some time the meaning of mother and father will have to be learned to them. Isn't that how they are taught now?"

When she heard this, she felt that it was right. Now Jodsna's present thinking is that English medium and entrance coaching etc. should be considered only after teaching the meritorious aspects of our culture and traditions first. However, we cannot ignore the flow of time. Jodsna is thinking again and envisaging a balanced education without spoiling good aspects of our culture along with modernity.

The entrance exam must be won for everything. Most parents are cautious about crossing their children that barrier. In the past, even if there was an influence of money, only those who had a natural interest in studying any professional course like medicine, etc. would go for it usually. They will benefit the society and him. But nowadays, before starting the education, parents decide the professional course for their children. Are these children being puppets to fulfill the ego of the parents?

School is closed for Onam. Both children spend most of their time in computer games. Jodsna bought some good children's magazines for them to develop reading habits. After two days, it is Thiruvonam. In the evening, they all went to town to buy some onamkodi (new dress). After getting new clothes, the children became happy and excited about Onam.

Onam holidays started at the office. Then her preparations for the Onam celebrations at home began to start. The rhythm of Onam's song and Onakali was becoming a charm for her. The remembrance of Onam celebrations in her childhood began to clear in her mind. In the evening, in the yard of the house on the north side, all the women from the neighborhood would gather to play onamkali there. They all together will sing songs, play, and watch the Onakali .. How nostalgic it is!

Two days before Jodsna had come back from the town after buying 'Trikakarayappan' and 'thumbachedi (2 things needed for rituals)'. Her husband is always very busy. He has no time for anything. On the day before onam when it was night, Jodsna decorated the car porch with ready-made items to welcome Onathappan as per rituals.

The children were watching TV. When they saw the scene of Vamana kicking Mahabali on the head on the screen, the children wondered each other.

'Isn't this nonsense'. The elder son is surprised.

'Luckily we were not living at that time'. The younger sister said.

Hearing this Jodsna said it is 'not like that, children' and started narrating the story to them, but they ignored it and continued watching TV.

She wanted to tell her children that Vamana Murthy, who blessed Mahabali by sending him to Suthalam (a place greater heaven) was born on the day of the month of Leo and that no one had trampled on Mahabali. But they had no interest in hearing that. The Glory of that influential force of which the universe, which is made up of five thatwas (five elements of the universe) Exists, is proclaimed through many stories in the Vedas and Upanishads. One of those stories is that of Vamanamoorthi and Mahabali. We are worshipping that magnificence of influence in different forms and different imaginations. Although we can see God's spirit in this, we know that they are not God. What a noble concept of God! Jodsna became more surprised and excited when she thought about it.

In any case, a realization started to take root in Jodsna that if we understand the culture and practices of our country and build a life according to it, along with academic study, children will have humility, simplicity, love, mutual understanding, etc. She was also convinced to pay more attention primarily to it. Then only after that, do we have to think about higher education like the professional course. Children should be monitored and let go their own way. Her husband also agreed with Jodsna's thinking. He said,

"If you have money in hand, it is a good way to get peace of mind by buying a small piece of land with natural beauty and start farming with a nice garden instead of giving it to educational vendors."

On Thiruvonam day, everyone got up early. Even though the children were not very interested, when they took a bath and put on their new clothes, they were also very excited. When she welcomed Onathappan with joy, along with her husband and children, her happiness was indescribable. At that time she recalled her memories and was thrilled with the occasion along with them.

"After the Onasadya(feast), let's go to the father's home, are you all ready?"Her husband asked them.

Upon hearing this, everyone again went into a celebratory mood. They all had their breakfast with joy, together with upper and sarkara puratti (snacks)which were bought from the shop, and poovada made by themselves. Then they hurriedly went to the kitchen to prepare the onam feast. feast.

....

A year-end Exam.

Sachin was sitting on the porch waiting for his son to come over after his year-end exam. When he slowly started to doze off due to the strong afternoon sun, he began to sink back into his childhood memories.

'The year-end exam is over. There is no need to listen to anyone's scolding anymore, no need to get beat by the teacher, no need to do homework. What a pleasure, wow! Sachin's mind started jumping with joy. As soon as he came home from school, he threw the book on the table. By that time, his mother had come with tea.

"How was the exam?" asked his mother.

"There was no problem, now it's peaceful. I have to play for a few days". Sachin said excitedly. While drinking tea, he was answering some of his mother's questions. After that, he jumped into the courtyard.

At first, he went to the foot of the mango tree that was grown up with a lot of branches spreading there. He threw stones at the mango tree and obtained three unripe mangoes which he ate biting with his teeth. When his sister came near, he gave one to her also.

There is a wide playground on the north side of his home. When the school is closed, all the children come and play there. Many friends come there to play daily. Hearing the sound of making plans to play somewhat there, he went to them.

"We were looking for you. Come on, we're going to play cricket." Someone told him loudly.

Meanwhile, someone took the mango from his hand. Januchechi's son Jayan is the oldest in that group. He is the leader who usually plays the game. Because of his leadership qualities or something, his opinion will be usually approved by all. He played with them till dusk. There was a lot of quarreling, fighting, and noise going on. After the game was over, everyone started going back to their homes. Even though it was dusk, no one in the house said anything to Sachin.

'Put the lamp. go and bathe, and chant god' Mother shouted from the kitchen.

After taking a minor bath himself, he chanted some prayers. Then he started to think about Mayavi, Kuttusan, luttapy, etc. to whom he had forgotten for some days as his mother hid those books due to his exam. So, he took his child's magazines, Balarama and Poompata, etc., and joined with his younger sister who was reading there. Her exam was just over. Now I have to read all the fables, Mulla's stories, and Aesop's stories. He thought. He found some books and read until fell asleep. He got a sound sleep after some days.

The next morning, a bunch of yellow konna flowers in the eastern courtyard like an all-blissful divine bride wearing all golden ornaments stands heralding Vishu's arrival. When he got up in the morning and sat on the porch wall, he suddenly turned his attention to that tree.

"Mom, is Vishu nearby?"

"Isn't it Vishu next week, don't you know?" Mother's reply.

Yes, He did not know. his brother and sister have never failed in any class. He also didn't want to have a failure. So, he studied hard without paying attention to anything else. As soon as he heard that it was Vishu, he got up and took the coins he had kept on the table and counted them. After taking it, he went outside and called Sasi.

"Come on Sasi, let's go to the north store and buy crackers."

Sasi, who studies in a lower class than him, will go along with whatever he says. There is no problem at his home either. Both of them went to the shop in the north and bought a small packet of crackers burst them put them in their playground and had fun.

His father came with a bundle of firecrackers on the day before Vishu. He was a brave man who used to light firecrackers holding in his hand and throw them away to burst. In the evening as soon as the lamp was lit, the packet of crackers was unwrapped.

" Tell everyone from inside to come". Father's order.

His father does not light the fireworks without my mother coming out from the kitchen. She is always in the kitchen busy preparing for Vishusadya(feast) etc. Hearing the father's order, everyone who was inside came to the threshold. The children of the neighborhood also came there running. For half an hour, everyone had fun lighting firecrackers, etc. His mother also lit poothiri.

"Children, look at your mother's face when she lights the poothiri." The father made fun of the mother. Right, the radiant face from long ago shone again in the light of the poothiri. His father enjoyed it!

Mother always goes to bed only after preparing vishukani (that which is seen first on Vishu) the day before. She had already picked a good kani cucumber from the southern yard before dusk.

All of his friends under the supervision of the leader Jayan have prepared a plan to show Vishukani in the early morning to all the houses. They are all excited about it. Sachin also wanted to join them. But his father wouldn't let him go. He went to bed with boredom. And fell asleep suddenly. It was about to dawn.

'Kanikanum neram kamalanethrante

kanakakingini ....'(song related to Lord Krishna))

His friends brought the kani and put it on their veranda. Then they moved aside by singing'kanikanum neram........'. He jumped up to hear the song. On a decorated chair there is a picture of an Unni Kannan and a lamp has been lit. He saw cucumbers, kasavu mundu, and coins on a plate. As his mother had told him, he folded his hands and prayed so that everyone would have all the virtues in the new year. His father put ten rupees on the plate. When he looked around, there were many friends. It was Jayan who was carrying the vishukani. He went with them up to the gate of the house and reluctantly came back. Vishukani had already been shown by his mother in the Brahma muhoortham itself by waking them by hiding their eyes. After that, the remaining firecrackers were also burst under the leadership of the elder brother.

"Everyone go and take a bath. After that Vishukaineetam (the first money given to the children by the elders on the day of Vishu) shall be given to all of you," said Mother.

By the time they came after taking a bath in the wide pond on the south side, their father after taking a bath had already sat on the armchair on the front side.

"Everyone comes here."

When they heard Father's voice, they went near to him. Each of them was given a one-rupee coin along with a 10 rupee note......'

Sachin was dreaming in sleep while waiting for his son Rahul to come out of school. Now he woke up from the dream. Suddenly he felt a sense of loss. That his father and mother are not with him today. All 3 siblings are also demised. He felt disappointed.

'If I could celebrate one more equinox with them and friends by playing, having fun bursting firecrackers, etc. just once.'He deeply wished in vain. A gasp? Tears fell from his eyes unknowingly.

Time will not go back. he calmed himself down after a while.

By that time he heard the sound of the school bus. This is the last day of his year-end exam. All the exams of his son are finished today. As soon as Rahul entered the home, he asked Sachin.

"Dad, my exam is over. Will you scold me if I play a video game now? I am very happy now."

"There is nothing wrong with playing a game. You should also pay attention to study well." He replied so because nowadays social media cannot be ignored in our daily lives. He continued again,

"The exam is over. Vishu is coming. Dad is thinking if we should go to the grandpa's house this year and celebrate with Cheriyacha's family there. what do you say?" Sachin expressed his desire and love to them.

"Won't we get bored, father?" His son is not interested after hearing this

Knowing the arrival of Rahul from the school, his wife got up from her afternoon nap and heard their talk. She said,

"It's fine to go. We should go the day before and return the same day. There are some good programs on TV, but we may miss them, why do you feel like this, this year?" His wife expressed her surprise.

"Oh, nothing. I just felt like it, never mind. We can go and come back the day before".

When he hears his wife's words, he doubts that his brother's family also might think in the same way. Time has gone and the past is past. Though it is hard to involve the change of time, it is inevitable. He calmed himself by thinking that this digital vision in this flat itself was enough, and asked his son about the details of the exam. Then he went inside with them to drink tea.

....

A Bangalore Trip.

I was traveling with my daughter on the train to Bangalore. There was no other problem because I had booked the seat in advance. There were people in all the seats. I kept my bags under the seat and on the berth and sighed. The train that was supposed to arrive at five o'clock arrived two hours late.

"Punctuality of time is needed not only for the railway but all of us have to be able to" Who said this? I had been bored with waiting on the platform. In any case, there is no such big problem for my daughter. She was sitting on the side seat looking at her mobile phone. So, the train whined and whistled and reached the next station. From there, many people got in with bundles and luggage. A woman came to my opposite seat. A familiar face in her. After a while, they looked at me and asked.

"Do you know me? Do you understand me?"

I know her and also I have seen her earlier. But I don't remember her name. Then I asked her,

" Are you the daughter of that brother who was running a ration shop in Alumparambu, I forgot his name".

"Yes, my name is Jolly and my father is Joseph. Where are you going?"

"We're going with a study affair for my daughter."

So, we both got to know each other. We were schoolmates. She had studied at the same school as me. Now she is a dance teacher. It was very nice to meet her. There is great pleasure for old people when they see people who were with them when they were young. That happiness is indescribable.

"Do you know one of my friends actress Santini? She is lying in the hospital without feeling well, I am going there. She is being treated in an Ayurvedic hospital."

I know the actress Shantini and have seen her in her youth. She was acting in drama in the early days. At that time, her marriage was not over. I have seen her father and mother go with her when they were going to act. They used to travel in front of our house she was known as" Kaitaram Shantini" at that time. She later acted in movies and became renowned. It can be said that the family life almost fell apart when she fell in love with someone who was acting with her. Later they separated and lived alone, but she got many opportunities in the movie.

Time passed and after that, I didn't know much about them except seeing them occasionally in movies.

"What is about her? Is she acting in movies and making much money?" I asked.

"Who said she has money? How much she struggled to get married to her daughter. She even borrowed from her co-stars. Later she couldn't act more."

Then I was surprised. I asked, "From the day I saw her, she had been acting in drama. yet hadn't she earned anything? Has not earned anything even though she has been in theatre and cinema for a long time?"

"If she had savings, would she have taken a loan?"Jolly replied.

Despite acting in films for many years, no matter how much I thought, I couldn't figure out what was the problem with her for her poverty. She even acted as the main actress in some films

"The women are underpaid. Especially to the supporting actresses."

"But then only men are enough in the movie." I felt angry.

Then my daughter, who was listening to our conversation, did not like my talk. She came close to me and told me.

"'Mom, shut up. Don't say anything unnecessary. Others are listening. We don't know the back story of the film industry. Why should we talk about things we don't know?'"

Then I scolded my daughter.

"We are old school friends; we know this actress. That's why we are talking about it. We don't need to know any backstory. She dedicated her life to art. At last, there is no one to look after her, and also has many loans. That's why I said so. There is nothing if whatever happened in the background."

Hearing the conversation between us Jolly laughed and spoke.

"My children also do not like to talk to anyone like this." I also laughed and continued in a low voice,

"Shouldn't all the actors be equally rewarded? If there is only a hero, then there won't be a movie. Don't need any other actors and actresses? Some people are capable and act with very interest. It is agreed. But the whole filmmakers themselves should give the effort to make the movie successful and lead them to huge rewards."

So, when we were talking about Santini in a low voice fearing my daughter, someone who was nearby said,

"Anyone interested can act if there is no shame in it. Unnecessary sense of morality and shame keep talented people away from this."

I thought it may be correct. In the past, we used to think that there were only very few singers in our state. Now, when all are getting the chance, we remember the gospel that 'the bigger is coming behind, don't stop him'.

Then I asked, "Does she get any help from the filmmakers".

"It is heard that their organization is giving away something small. She said.

.   Unfortunately, some people who have acted for five or ten years earn a lot and even do charity work with their surplus earnings. She may also get some kind of generosity from them.

"Shouldn't the wide gap between the main actor and others be ended? The industry itself should think about it. If the script, direction, and make-up are good, the movie will be successful. If there is a good actor, it will be a little better. Why don't these main actors act in bad films? then their audience will leave them. Isn't it?"Their success depends on the quality of the film.

I revealed the disparities prevailing in the industry as I understand. The industry itself is making them celebrities for its promotion. As

Jolly is a dance teacher they are close friends. That is why she is interested in discussing all these matters.

"If the film is good as a whole, full credit will be given to the actors, especially to the main actor. They are the ones whom the people see directly. The poor viewers do not know those who worked behind the scenes."

"That means the heroes are lucky stars.?".

"Yes, That's the same. The main actors earn cash on the audience's ignorance. Creative writers also see the light through them. Isn't it"

"Couldn't this be why it is called an enlightened state? I told them ironically. Then continued,

"Let it all go, how is she doing now?"

". Now it's going on like this, it will take a long time to get better. She will have to sell the house in the end to get out of there."

When I heard that, I felt very sad. I spoke.

"This disparity in the film industry should be ended. There should be a limit on the remuneration for the heroes and co-stars. Everyone is doing the same job. Like the boss in an office, there is no responsibility for the work of colleagues."

So, by the time our discussion got intense, the train reached Palakkad.

When her friend excitedly held her hand and said goodbye, her daughter captured the scene on her mobile phone. Then they took their bags and got down at the station. By that time, the tea boy on the train came with tea. We each bought tea and drank it. The procession of these tea-boys happens when there is no room to stand in the general compartment. I have often felt that is it not enough to allow them in at least between a gap of half an hour. If we see some people, it seems that they are boarding the train to eat only.

Several passengers were boarding from Palakkad. Another person reached into her seat. If we get acquainted with her, we can understand many other stories. The train started moving slowly.

....

A Chit Chat.

"Didn't you know that the marriage of the daughter of our Balan is fixed?"Santhamma asked my mother from the kitchen yard.

My mother and this Santhamma have been friends for years. Santhamma's husband, Shankunni, does not go to work regularly. They were earning their livelihood by rearing cows and other things. When they got old, they stopped raising cows after marrying off their two daughters. However, she used to talk to my mother about all the news. My mother Leela was also very eager to hear what Santhamma said.

"Oh well. How much he struggled to live. Now he is beginning to escape. He had been in the Gulf earlier for a long time, isn't he?

"That's right," Santhamma shook her head. The mother continued.

"Both girls are smart to look at. They have good character and education. Anyone will like them. I had known they were planning for that. Anyway, it's good. Where are they going to marry their child?"

Mother is anxious. The face spread like a flower.

"It is heard that the boy is working in IT. His daughter has completed an MBA."

Santhamma was telling her all the details that she knew. Despite her age, my mother and she have no major health problems. I suddenly remembered the scene where one-day Santhamma came to tell her about Baletan's wedding affairs when I was studying in the 4th class in school or something like that.

One Afternoon, the mother was sitting leaning against the wall of the veranda on the west side of the house and resting. There is always a smile on her face, which is hidden only when she sleeps. What makes her dear to everyone is the smile on her face. At that time, Santhamma came to tie the goat in the field. She is young. She comes here in her leisure time to chat with my mother occasionally. She sat on the veranda putting her legs to the yard with her mother.

"Balan the son of our janakichechi has come from the Gulf now. It is said that he is searching for a girl to marry."Santhamma started talking. Mother was also eager to know her today's story.

Santhamma has a lot of chickens and goats, and her job is to raise them. She was going here and there around the fields with her goats to feed them. She will not leave anyone in her sight without any talk. While feeding the goats, she holds everyone who passes by and talks to them. The task of conveying all the information she got to my mother without leaving a trace was continuing without any special orders from anyone. Mother had many special affections for her sheep and it was her custom to take and keep fruit peels etc. to give them. Santhamma was quite fat and tall with black curly hair. The end of the front part of her blouse was always seen open without using a safety pin there.

"What's the matter, Aren't there two girls? Why do they try to marry him before them?" the mother shared her concern.

"They want to see him get married. They say, 'The girls have studied well, let them find a job'. What can we say? It is correct. Let the girls find their livelihood to live in their own will. Neighbours say that now Januchechi is very proud after his arrival."

In the meantime, Mother extended to her the betel pot. After chewing the betel and talking for a while, she left. Santhamma has to come to my mother to spend her leisure time joyfully.

It had been two years since Balan went to the Gulf. Although he had passed his pre-degree, as his father died, he had to stop his studies and work in his uncle's shop. It was a time when common people started earning money by going to Persia. That's how Balan started to feel the lust of the Gulf. He said to his mother one day.

"Mom, there is no gain in going to this shop and working. There is no chance of getting a government job at present. I am thinking of going to Persia...shall I go? How will I make money?"

'If we go to Makkah, we will get a handful of gold, but we have to go to Makka.' That was her inner feeling. However, she gave her son full support.

"So, if you have such a fate, I can't stop you. Go to see the Gulfkaran (nickname of a Pravasi) you mentioned and ask him if he can arrange to get a visa."

Thus, that mother and her son also got to know an agent through the Gulfkaran. It was a fraud. Without realizing that, they borrowed all the money to go to Gulf and went to Bombay.

"Janakichechi sent her son to Persia by serving in the house of that Gulfkaran."

When Santhamma came to fetch porridge water for the goats, she told her mother secretly. Baletan's mother had already told my mother and knew all the matters. So, the conversation did not last long. Soon Balan went to the Gulf. Santhamma is a regular visitor of the Baleton's house as well as here.

"I have told Janakichechi that like our Devassi, she should try to tear down the house, rebuild it, and arrange weddings for her children."

She brags about how she taught Janakichechi to spend money. It is because of such unnecessary discussions that he could not earn much. That poor man wandered around in Bombay for about a month. Then he followed the Gulfkaran and somehow reached there.

He went to the gulf dreaming of a high salary and a good standard of living. But he had to reach a small company on top of a mountain with a low salary. Unfortunately, he had also to work under the sun's heat. Then he blamed the decision to go there. However, there was some relief. Anyway, he didn't have to return from Bombay. Thus, his miserable life as an expatriate began there.

He would send money every month. it will be enough to pay the debt and the daily expenses. Mother used to wait for the arrival of the postman to get a letter. if there is a registered letter, the postman will be very happy. He knows that it will be a cheque. In its happiness, she will give something to the postman. In this way, anyhow he completed two years. Now Santhamma is telling her about his return by sitting on the veranda with her.

He borrowed some gold and money from one of his friends. When she writes a letter to her son, she always reminds him of his wedding. Thus, one day a car came in front of his house and he got out of it with some luggage of clothes, make-up materials, a tape recorder, etc. My mother was the first to see him.

"Balan has come with putting two boxes tied on the top of the car," said the mother to everyone in the house.

The next day, when Santhamma went to see him, she was given a foreign soap. she also heard the gulf details. Then it was like a festival there. Whoever entered there, would open and show the box that was brought. Both the girls started going to the temple wearing foreign sarees. Hindi songs were flowing from the tape recorder. Janakichechi was busy always. In the meantime, the search for a girl also started.

Everyone began to look at Balan with great admiration. Because the Gulf has become a place to make money for everyone, especially to the unskilled workers. Eusep's son Devassi, who was unemployed with no education and no money, went to the Gulf to earn money as a stonemason. He could earn much and married his sister Annie to a rich man. He demolished his old two-room house and built a big house. After some time, he bought the land around the house and added it to the house. He also married a beautiful girl. Though the Gulf was a place to make money, it also required luck. All those who go to the Gulf do not get the same luck.

Even though Balan did not have much savings, he did not have any shortage of pride. His uncle proposed to him to marry the daughter of a rich man. Even though he had no money, he was handsome and good-natured, so they liked him very much. Thus, that marriage was conducted with borrowed money. After marriage again he went back to the Gulf.

Later it was a paper marriage' for about a year. Phones were very rare in those days. In the early days, people like Balan had gone and built up the gulf that is seen today. Today's generation is going and experiencing it.

Thus, while continuing with that job, he realized that the salary he was getting would be nothing and he took up a job on his own without permission. While doing that, the police caught him and it is said that he returned home with his luck. Someone who was with him in the

Gulf told this information there. Santhamma secretly told this to my mother and wondered about the loss of his work.

"Leeledathi, even if a cat comes home, it will have luck., won't it?"Mother became indifferent without giving any reply.

After that, the lives of his siblings changed completely. If we lose anything outside, don't we react with our mother at home? Then Balan became isolated from the family and started to live only looking after his affairs. He hesitated to go back to his old job and tried many other jobs. In the meantime, two daughters were born too. Due to the luck of those children, he got a small permanent job from the Public Service Commission Thus, he got some relief for his sufferings. He taught her children well. Now the eldest is under proposal to marry.

When the love and care of Balan began to be lost, the lives of his mother and siblings became miserable which was moving in a different direction. It became a different story,

Now Santhamma is still standing in the yard.

"Don't stand there and come inside". Mother invited her to sit.

"What is being given to the girl as dowry?" Mother was in a hurry to know that.

"They didn't ask anything. I heard that there are 30 Pawans in their hand. Although it was late, he got a government job and he escaped. But life is very difficult for the other children and Janakichechi now."After saying this, Santhamma was about to leave again.

"Don't you go, let's have a glass of tea." 'The mother insisted again. She agreed and stepped up to the veranda.

....

A Different Complacency.

Ramettan slowly walked along the side of the paddy field which ends in a pathway. If we walk a little along that path, we will reach a big house. As soon as he reached there by walking, he began to get excited he stretched his legs and walked fast. Stepping on the cobblestones, he reached the gate of that big house. He became very happy to get there. It is his younger sister Vimala's house. There is no one on the porch. It feels a little like an empty atmosphere there. On a mat, paddy is drying in the yard. He pressed his finger on the calling bill.

Although it was his sister's house, he had not come here for a long time. Now he has come to invite his son's wedding. It is a holiday, so he came today thinking that everyone would be there at home. Since his sister and her husband are employees, he will not see anyone there on weekdays. Both children will go to study.

"Ah, Rametta, come and sit". Vimala's husband Vishwam opened the door and invited him lovingly. Ramanadhan is his brother-in-law and it seems that he had expected such an arrival. He took water from the kindi (a pot) placed on the porch, washed his feet, and entered inside.

"Are you tired from walking?" As soon as Vimala saw him, she enquired about his wellness. She felt very happy to see him.

"As I walked along the field with a pleasant breeze, I didn't feel tired." He spoke.

Then Vimala went to the kitchen and came with tea. Along with that, her two children also came around and started talking. They were overjoyed to see their uncle. While sharing their family affairs and discussing the wedding details, Vimala got up and went to the kitchen. She brought a big mango after cutting it into pieces. It was very sweet and big like a coconut and they all enjoyed its sweetness.

"It was unnecessary to come here to invite us, even if you hadn't come, we would have been there."

Hearing these words from Viswam, he thought. 'If I don't say this now, his reaction may be otherwise'. Anyway, he replied,

"Oh, it doesn't matter."

After having tea and inviting, Rametan went down to the yard and looked at her house and surroundings. He saw an areca nut tree garden, the hayloft, the cowshed, etc. there. Vishwam and his children also joined him. Different kinds of vegetables like tapioca, banana, mango tree, jackfruit tree, and okra have made the whole field green. An affluent home with an antiquity. These are all the result of the efforts of his ancestors. But don't you feel a void somewhere? 'It is the satisfaction and joy of a woman that becomes the light of any home.' he thought to himself. When he got up to leave after some resting, Vimala said.

"Let's go tomorrow bro, it's been a while after here, isn't it?" Vishwam also supported her.

On hearing this, Ramettan thought for a while. 'In any case, I came here only after a long. Now I am tired of going to many houses. Therefore, it is better to stay here today. Then he said,

"There are some more places I have to go. But if that is your desire, well, let it be so."

By the time Vimala heard that, she became very excited. He is her elder brother who is responsible for protecting her. But she has such a husband who does not give her and her children a chance to get that protection and love from them.

As she was happy to have her elder brother there, quickly got ready to change his dress and prepare the bed to rest for him. When all the housework was done, she came alone and asked him about her mother and household details. Later, she began to pour out her complaints and frustrations. He listened to all with indifference because he knew everything about him already. Viswam is always so and has not changed. No one will talk to him about her complaints. There is no matter in talking.

It was evening. Then everyone sat there watching TV and talking about the local things for a while. Vishwam mostly talked about the difficulty of farming. In between Vimala's disobedience was also mentioned by him. Ramettan did not pretend to hear it. Soon everyone had dinner and went to their respective places to sleep. At that time Ramettan and Vishwam were sitting on that settee for a while and began to talk about their old matters.

After a while, Vishwam got up and went to the kitchen. He was then sitting there alone for a while watching and listening to their life. Then he began to think. How clever was his sister Vimala? She was mostly in the field of social and cultural activities. She studied well and got a job but what's the matter, the partner she got, is a person without any virtues. He loves only his possessions and has only his likes and dislikes in life. Just like a mechanical life. He has no interest in any external matters like art and literature etc. It is his opinion that all artists are said to be starving. But both children are good-natured and obedient to him. As they have grown up seeing his rigid nature, they accept his orders without any hesitations.

So, thinking about all these things, he was reclining on that settee and slowly fell into a stupor. During his stupor, the images of Viswam and Vimala began to flash in his mind......

'He is checking the kitchen.it is 10.15 pm. It's always like that. His own house. Shouldn't he keep it? What if his wife gets careless?

Even the Bus ticket, which he had got while traveling on the bus during his studies, had been stacked on his desk for a long period. Viswam knows some electrical repair and his house is full of useless electrical pieces of equipment. Even if anyone comes to pick them up, he does not give it. He is keeping each and everything considered as valuable as gold. He needs everything. If any beggars come, he will not even hesitate to drive them away. It is his habit to keep the windows and doors of the house always shut safely.

'If we have money, we can live. These days, there is nothing great in speaking morality'. This is his principle of life and without saying loudly he is trying to teach this to his children also. He has a special ability to keep the children close to him by keeping her relatives at a distance. Vimala is just the opposite to it and doesn't like any of his habits or practices.

"Why don't you give unnecessary things if there are people who need them?" He asked her once.

"No one will ask for anything here. Even if anyone comes, he won't give them. Then he will tell like this, 'I don't want to feed anyone. I have not made a plan to feed everyone. If they do not have anything, it is their fate. What do I need for that? I want to enjoy what God has given me. I will not give it to anyone.' What can I do then?"

After hearing her answer, he said nothing more. He also has a job with a good monthly salary, goes to work punctually, and meets the necessary expenses with the income he gets. He is strict in all matters. Since his father does not have any job, he has the responsibility of looking after his parents and siblings. He is very eager to spend for the family without his wife knowing. It can be said that he does not have a world outside except his own home.

"I don't want anything from anyone, and no one needs to expect anything from me." This is his other policy. He doesn't even like anyone except his family to come to that house, especially those who need some kind of help. That's why anyone from her family doesn't come here very often.

Vimala is lucky since she has a job and an income. She mostly takes care of all the household expenses. If she wants to use something according to her preferences, she has to buy it herself. Like a cat blindfolded and drinking milk, after using all her savings in any manner there, he will say without any reluctance, 'Have I asked for any of your money?'

That's right, if she asks for any money to spend after giving her salary to him, he will throw it away in anger. So, she began to spend herself. After enjoying all her savings, he behaves towards her in the manner of 'You have nothing here, everything is mine.' Being arrogant, she can't say anything against him. His nature is mostly exploited by his sister and husband showering love on him. Poor, my sister! How is she suffering all this? What would have been her life if she hadn't any of her income?

Even though he is like that at home, he is decent outside. He doesn't talk too much and is a bad person when he gets angry. Many people who know him closely are afraid of him. When it is thought about it, it's true. Aren't the words of those who don't talk much more powerful?'

Thus, thinking about him one by one, while dozing on the settee Vimala came to him and knocked gently. He suddenly got up from his slumber.

Vishwam checked the doors, and the gate several times and went to sleep after ensuring safety. He is keeping everything without any purpose. It is not known why this is so. As for Vimala, she lives her life doing her matters without paying any attention to them. He takes care of his 'possessions' and achieves self-satisfaction! Fortunately, although he gives no satisfaction to his wife, he is careful about his children and also very satisfied with himself. Different expressions of satisfaction!!

Vimala had already prepared sleeping facilities in the living room. A beautiful bed sheet. Water in a jug for drinking. All facilities are available. he took a glass of water and drank. Then he went to sleep.

Despite there is everything, life was just boring because he didn't know how to behave properly. Who can advise Vishwam? He turned around, pulled the blanket over him, and started to sleep by thinking again about the fate of his beloved sister who tries to find satisfaction in gardening, etc..and her husband who finds self-satisfaction in his selfishness and ego.

....

Intercity.

Athirakutty is the youngest daughter of Raghavan Kaimal and Meenakshi Amma. After completing her PG from Maharajas College, while Athira was staying at home, her parents became busy getting her married and started searching for marriage proposals. After taking the matrimonial site and registering the profile, her father started to check this site for a good bridegroom. It was then that one day her mother told her that someone was coming to see her. When she heard it, she became very worried and went to her mother and said.

"Mom, only after I get a job, I will be ready for the wedding. Don't think about anything now."

"I want to go for coaching for a bank test. I have to get a job. how should I live without a job at this time Mom?" she said again.

Mother had no objection to her opinion. She spoke.

"Okay, you need a job. Meanwhile, if any good proposal comes along with it, then it can be done. Now go for coaching."

"Mom, no one wants to see me now."She said again.

She later went to her father and insisted. Thus, that idea stopped there. She is right. Instead of asking for dowry in the past, now even poor families are also seeking girls who have jobs and their income.

Anyway, Athira started going for bank coaching. Later, as she passed the bank test with a high rank, she was selected as an assistant manager and joined the Bank of Baroda branch at Palakkad. It was there that she met Sreenath the neighbour of her mother's home as her subordinate. He was the son of Rajalakshmi of the Sreenilayam, the house on the south side there.

"Good morning, madam, don't you know me?"

"Oh, I know. Aren't you from the Sreenilayam? What about your parents? So, they renewed their acquaintance.

Although they knew each other, they had not spoken till today. There is a little mischief of God that Athira was able to become the superior of Sreenadh. What is that? Let's go back to Athira's childhood to find out.

She is studying in LP school. During school vacation, Athira will be at her mother's house. There is a grandmother, uncle, aunt, and their children living there. After vacation there, she returns only when school opens. She spends the whole day playing with her uncle's children and walking behind her grandmother. At night, they all tell stories, sing songs, etc. She is sleeping in the room on the south side of the house. Grandma would be with her for all their mischief. Uncle and aunt say that Grandmother has twice as much energy when reaches Athiramol. Those days with her grandmother are a treasure trove of memories.

If the window is opened from the bedroom while they are lying on the bed, it can be seen the Sreenilayam, the home of Sreenadh in the south. When it is dawn no one in the house will awake except her grandmother. Then the light from the kitchen of that house on the south will begin to start filtering in through the window glass of the room. If lie down and pay attention there it can be heard the sound of bathing there. Sometimes they can hear the voice of his mother saying, "Take a bath, child," and "Don't stir the water in the pond, children, etc." There is a big pond in the kitchen area for bathing for them. It is surrounded by silky sandy soil and the water is green with small moss.

As soon as his mother Rajalakshmi gets up, she goes to the pond first. After taking a bath changing her clothes and soaking dirty clothes in soap, she will enter inside. She will not enter the kitchen without taking a bath. Each morning there begins with the children and husband taking a bath first. By the time the day time comes, everyone except grandmother will become 'garden fresh'. The maid will come and wash all the soaked clothes later. Bathing, Thevaram, Sandhyavandanam, and Murajapa(rituals) are the parts of their daily routine.

Before the break of dawn, the pleasure of taking a bath in the pond in that pleasant atmosphere is different. The sound of their bathing and some' kalapilas sounds' often wake up Athira in the morning.

When she gets up and sits on the veranda on the east side, it can be seen that Sreenath the elder son in that house going to the temple along the road in front of the house with a small steel bucket full of flowers. Sometimes he may be accompanied by his brother Harish, and sometimes his sister Shobha. Then it will be almost six o'clock. The three of them were walking looking down without letting anyone speak. Her aunt secretly calls him Mr. 'Keezhottunokki'(one who looks down). It is a pleasure for her to see them walking to the temple in that early morning.

This sreenilayam is a big old ancestral home. Sreenath's grandmother with grandma's mother and her sister and also with an uncle used to live there many years ago. There was a young man called Raman Nair as a cook in the kitchen at that time for making food for them. He was very beautiful and any woman would look at him. He had a well-developed chest, a full body with enough height, and a very humble speech. He also had a special skill in preparing delicious food. After looking at him, Grandma's younger sister Malathikutty fell in love with the cook. The commotion there was indescribable when the relationship was known and immediately the cook was sent away. Grandmother began to advise her beloved sister.

"Marry a soodran? Shiva Shiva! Caste, what is his work, what is there in his house? Let that go too, does he know the murajapam or Thevaram, etc.? What the Soodras had been told to do, do you know that, child? what is their clan work? The child should forget him."

Caste was not a problem for them. He is a poor cook and has no money. How can they tolerate this? Malathikutty is now desperate and has no bath, no food, and no sleep. She always spends her time sitting idle and lying in the kitchen and Patthayapura. They did everything they could to break this relationship. But there was no change for Malathikutty. Finally, she said.

"Okay, I don't want to get married, but don't force me to get married again."

And so, the months went on. The Cook after going from there started a grocery. Everyone thought that the chapter was over. Malathikutty began to go to the temple as usual. But it was another beginning. He would come when she was going to the temple. They started seeing each other again. Finally, one day she went down with him. This is the story of Grandma's sister. Later they came there only when her grandmother died. Uncle and his family had also gone to his wife's house.

Sreekuttan's grandmother is an old woman with hair like a cotton ball. Her husband died earlier. Her regular attire is a white rauka(a blouse)and a small mundu. She has three children. The eldest daughter lives in Vadakara. The second daughter Rajalakshmi and her husband and children are with her. Rajalakshmi's husband works in the High Court. Their children are Sreekuttan, Harikutan and Shobha.

Athira's mouth still waters when she remembers how she used to pick mangoes from the yard in the south of their home during the mango season, put them in her clothes, add salt, and eat them all. If anyone goes there, it can be seen that there are full of trees, plants, and flowers everywhere., and one can also feel god's blessings with the presence of noble and punctual people there. If the eldest daughter's children also arrive at the time of school vacations, then there is a big celebration.

When her grandma usually goes to the Sreenilayam, she does not enter directly and goes to the west veranda through the south side. When she was there, the insiders would also come. Then by sitting on the veranda, their talking would be started. If they see Athira, they will say,

"Isn't this child Saraswati's daughter? Same face." Then she will shake her head.

Then some sweets will be brought and given to her. Athira would sit with her grandmother for some time listening to her story. Then she would gather leaves, pick mangoes, pick mints from hedges, and all that she could do in the yard.

It is a nice wide sandy yard. She wants to run and play in the yard but there is no one will come with her. The children there do not come down to play with her. They interact with those coming from outside by stopping them in the yard. If they too came down to the yard, it would be fun to play! But they will come to the door and stand there just staring at her. Lakshmana Rekha! In the past, it was grandma's family members who had washed their clothes. That's why they behave like that. She was told by her grandmother when she asked about it. They would return happily after buying some presents like mangoes or jack fruit etc. that his mother would give her for bringing home.

Thus, Athira's childhood was a time when Sreekuttan and his family were treated with great respect by all. Later, when she entered high school and college, she did not go to her mother's home to stay.

In the meantime, Sreekuttan studied and passed his MBA. He got a job at Palakkad Bank. He is always going from Thrissur to Palakkad by train. Season tickets have been taken by him. Mother will prepare all the food in the morning and give it to him in a tiffin box. Even though his grandmother is old, she has not lost any seriousness. She is still the one who is in charge of the household administration, and when the sun goes down, they clean and polish the chandeliers to light them.

Sreekuttan still goes to the temple in the morning. On the days he does not go, his mother will allow him to leave the house only after praying in the puja room. When the train reaches Thrissur, many people will get off. Then they will get a seat for sure. There is always a big group to go to work on this train along with him. Mostly they all will occupy the same compartment.

Now he is not that Keezhottunoki Sreenadh whom we had met so far on the journey! They are all talking with jokes and bursts of laughter. They will discuss all under the sun including office matters, top trending news, etc. there. Once the train Shornur arrives, it is only their world.

It is very nice to see some of the officers in that group bring the morning breakfast wrapped and eat it sitting face to face on the train and sharing the news. Maria Fernandes is one of them. She always comes after having breakfast. But she always keeps a packet in her hand. Everyone will take and eat it. She is unmarried and works in the water authority department. Good eloquence. She has a piece of knowledge about anything. Her golden complexion, round glasses, long hair, soft body like a flower, and above all her knowledge made her the darling of the group. Sreekuttan and she are good friends. Even after getting off the train, both of them have to go in the same direction. Thus, they became eternal companions. It is his habit to hold a seat for Maria or to find a seat next to him when she is far away. Now without her, he has no fun and gets bored.

After some time, both of them fell deeply in love. Realizing the depth of the flow of love in their snehathoni(boat of love), they finally decided to get married.

Maria didn't face any big opposition in her house. But if we talk about him? It can be said that they were very conservative. All the things that took place in that house after that are indescribable. All the routines were gone in that house. There was only one time meal for days. For a month everyone there did not even speak to each other. Sreekuttan is talking only to his father now. Despite all this, Sree was not ready to give up. He said with a firm decision.

"If you don't agree, I will marry her by registration, I will bring her here and make her stay."

It can be said that they accepted his threat. With that, they agreed him to the marriage. Thus, the marriage was conducted in a nearby hall. Only the very indispensable relatives of Sreenadh attended the function.

Sreenath's family, who used to keep outsiders and especially other castes in their yard, now live with a Christian girl named Maria Fernandes. ....

After getting up early in the morning, after taking a bath and Thevaram, Sri will still go to the temple. On Sunday, he will also go to church with Mary. When they decided to get married, they had made a promise to each other.

"Sree can live according to your customs, but I have to go to church on Sunday. It is compulsory for me."

"Surely, I will take you."

Sree agreed. It was an agreement between them. Even if Shri is told to change his religion, maybe he will agree. Now in front of him, there is only her smile which shines like a rainbow.

Months passed by. There is no wound that time heals. The family's opposition to her started to reduce. Maria began to like the new life. She started enjoying their rituals, Kavu, temple, Tulasithara, etc. She changed her name to 'Meera Sreenath' according to her own choice and started following Sree's way of life. Now Sreenadh and Meera are going together to the temple.

"There is no place for caste or religion in our life, as long as there is love. There is no lack of love here." This is what his mother says when anyone talks about this relationship.

"She lives the same way as here. If the way of life is accepted, life can be comfortable in any religion," Grandmother also comforted herself by saying so. Anyway, their married life is moving forward strongly. With everyone's blessings!

Thus, Sreenadh the member of that orthodox family, whom Athira's family called by the name Keezhotunokki in her childhood and who kept her away by not allowing her to enter his home and also who kept outsiders in their yard is now working as her subordinate after marrying from a different religion! What can be said except for a small mischievous shown by God during the train journey?

....

Heaven and Hell.

This is an old story.

One day Bhagavan (Lord) was resting in Vaikundam. Then a cry was heard from somewhere. Bhagavan noticed where it was coming from. Then Bhagavan immediately realized that the crying was coming from hell. Immediately Bhagavan went to hell to find out what was going on there. Then several inhabitants of hell came running to Bhagavan and grabbed Bhagavan's feet saying to save them from this hell and started praying loudly.

All the sights seen there were very pitiful. In many places, the trees were cut and dried up. In some places, the rivers dried up and people were wandering for drinking water. in some other places, the hills and mountains were destroyed. Cracked roads and leaking pipes were seen all over there. Nature also through its emanating vibration is disturbing living creatures. As the Garbage is piled up, people are walking with their noses covered, and the atmosphere is fully polluted. Oxygen is bought for breathing on one side whereas in some places thirsty water is bought and drank in bottles. Garbage like plastic is piled up and burnt. Charcoal, toxic smoke, and traffic jams were seen in most of the places.

All people are lifestyle patients. On one side nature is destroyed and on the other side, some people are harassing, attacking, and murdering each other. Bhagavan saw all kinds of sinners, such as truth-breakers, embezzlers, false witnesses, gold thieves, idol thieves, and adulterers. Everywhere there was news of corruption, cruelty, and iniquity. When they saw Bhagavan, the people of hell cried loudly saying,

"It is not right that you left many people to enjoy in heaven and only us to this hell, Lord. We are tired of hell. We also want heavenly happiness."

Hearing all this, Bhagavan took pity on them and pacified them.

From there, Bhagavan immediately went to heaven and looked there. What a beautiful sight he saw there!

Everyone was happily enjoying their lives themselves. What a peaceful and holy atmosphere. It was seen everywhere that lotus flowers bloom in beautiful freshwater lakes, and many kinds of trees of different ages and sizes full of beautiful ripe fruits, and flowers are seen everywhere., Birds like flamingos, parrots, peacocks, etc. fly in groups. Blackbuck deer along with fierce animals like buffalo, lion, etc. are living together without fear. All are living comfortably in great palaces similar to golden palaces. Nowhere is the worship of God or Bhakti. It is only when one is in sorrow that there comes a need to invoke God. Here all are God-like with all the virtues sharing blessings without even the fear of death and living happily and contented. There is only purity, love comfort, peace, and prosperity everywhere. Wow! Where When the Lord came to hell, he had to see the people who were affected by evil feelings like lust, greed, drunkenness, nepotism, cruelty injustice, etc.

Bhagavan told the people of heaven about the plight and complaints of the people of hell. He asked them to go to hell for a few days and give heaven to the people of hell. Aren't the people of heaven used to giving only? They agreed. Thus the inhabitants of hell, who were accustomed only to receive, reached heaven. The inhabitants of heaven reached hell also.

It's been a while. Bhagavan started hearing the crying again. Then the Lord thought that the people of heaven were crying in hell because they were not familiar with this life of hell. But it was from heaven. Bhagavan wondered why they were crying in heaven. When Bhagavan looked there anxiously, he saw nothing of the golden palaces or flower-strewn paths that were there before.

They all collided with each other and smashed and collapsed everything. Streams and rivers were polluted. Roads were broken up. Mountains and hills were broken. It was just like the old hell they had been through. Bhagavan asked,

"What's wrong here?'"

"Lord, when they got to heaven and came here, everyone became very arrogant and egotistic. No one knows what to say or do. Please, Lord, it is enough, transfer us to our old place "Saying this they started crying again. Bhagavan was again confused but decided to transfer them to hell.

But when he went there, he could not see hell there. The people of heaven went there and buried all the garbage and cleaned the rivers, and the atmosphere became clean due to the effect of their sacred spiritual radiance. Clean air, clean water, clean soil, and good food and drinks were abundant there. Then Bhagavan gathered the inhabitants of heaven and hell together and gave a counsel.

"Heaven and hell are not getting free for anyone. It must be earned by our effort. The only thing required for it is our attitude. To change the attitude, a noble mindset is required. Thought is the seed of any action. Therefore, the effort to make our mind, intellect, and understanding noble and pure is more urgent than efforts for material gains."

Having said this, the Bhagavan returned from there.

....

About the Author

Renuka.K.P.

Smt.Renuka.K.P. is a native of Ernakulam district of Kerala state as a daughter of Late Sri.Parameswaran and Late Smt.Kousalia. After her graduation she entered into Kerala govt. service and retired as Tahsildar. Now she is actively engaged as an online writer and clearly exhibits her outlook on social and cultural affairs of the society, especially against domestic violence of women.

www.ingramcontent.com/pod-product-compliance
Lightning Source LLC
LaVergne TN
LVHW041638070526
838199LV00052B/3430